LUCY DANIELS

Little Animal Ark™

The Fearless Fox

Hodder
Children's
Books

A division of Hachette Children's Books

Special thanks to Narinder Dhami

Little Animal Ark is a trademark of Working Partners Limited
Text copyright © 2003 Working Partners Limited
Created by Working Partners Limited, London, W6 0QT
Illustrations copyright © 2003 Georgie Ripper
Cover illustration copyright © 2003 Andy Ellis

First published in Great Britain in 2003 by Hodder Children's Books

This edition published in 2007

The rights of Lucy Daniels and Georgie Ripper to be identified as the author
and illustrator of this work respectively have been asserted by them in
accordance with the Copyright, Designs and Patents Act 1988.

1

A Catalogue record for this book is available from the
British Library

ISBN-13: 978 0 340 93260 5

Printed and bound in Great Britain by
Clays Ltd, St Ives plc

The paper and board used in this paperback by Hodder Children's
Books are natural recyclable products made from wood grown in
sustainable forests. The manufacturing processes conform to the
environmental regulations of the country of origin.

Hodder Children's Books
A division of Hachette Children's Books
338 Euston Road, London NW1 3BH
An Hachette Livre UK Company

Chapter One

"Weren't the kittens lovely?" Mandy Hope said happily to her mum. "The black and white one was my favourite. She was so friendly."

Her mum smiled as she drove the Land-rover down the winding country lane. "I could tell you liked her," she said.

Mandy's parents were both vets. Today Mrs Hope and Mandy

had gone to visit Mrs Owen, who lived outside Welford in a pretty country cottage. Mrs Owen's cat had just had four kittens.

The Hopes lived at Animal Ark in Welford, and the surgery where Mandy's mum and dad worked was at the back of their cottage. That meant there were always animals around. Mandy thought that she was the luckiest girl in the world!

"When will the kittens' eyes open?" Mandy asked.

"In a week or two," replied her mum.

Mandy hoped that she would be able to see the kittens again

when they were a bit bigger. She looked out of the window. The sun was warm in the cloudless blue sky. The woods on either side of the road were leafy and green. It was Saturday so Mandy wasn't at school, and very soon it would be the summer holidays.

She'd have even more time to play with the kittens then!

Suddenly Mandy noticed that the silver car in front of them was slowing down. Mrs Hope braked sharply. Mandy gasped as she was jolted in her seat.

Mrs Hope frowned. "Are you OK, Mandy?" she asked. "I don't know what that driver is doing."

Mandy stared at the silver car.

It had stopped in the middle of the road. The driver had stuck his head out of the window and was staring at something in front of his car.

"Oh!" Mandy exclaimed, pointing. "There's a fox!"

The fox was trotting across the road just in front of the silver car. He had thick, reddish-coloured fur and a long bushy tail with a white tip.

He stopped and looked curiously at the cars with his bright dark eyes. He didn't seem scared at all! Then he trotted to the other side, jumped over the ditch, and disappeared into the trees.

"Oh!" Mandy said in delight. She'd never seen a fox so close before. "Was it a baby? He didn't look very big."

"He was certainly young," replied Mrs Hope. "But he looked old enough to leave his mother."

"He didn't look very scared of the cars," Mandy said. "He must be really brave."

"That's not a good thing," said her mum with a frown.

"A fox needs more road safety sense than that!"

Mandy stared out of the window of the car as they drove on again. She felt excited as she remembered the fox's white-tipped tail and shining dark eyes. She tried to spot him again among the trees, but he had vanished into the undergrowth.

Chapter Two

Mandy put her satchel down on a chair and went into the waiting room. It was Monday, and she'd just got back from school. "Hello, Jean," she said to the receptionist.

Jean Knox turned to smile at Mandy. She was sorting through leaflets in the corner of the empty room. "Hello, Mandy," she said. "Would you like to help me tidy these up?" She pointed at the leaflets, which were all about caring for different kinds of pets.

"I'd love to!" Mandy said. She picked up some leaflets about cats and put them in a neat pile. "Peter's coming here with Timmy this afternoon.

He told me at school." Peter Foster was in Mandy's class. He owned a Cairn terrier pup called Timmy.

"That's right," said Jean. "It's time for Timmy's booster injections. Perhaps there's not much point in tidying up if he's on his way!"

Mandy laughed. Timmy loved making a mess! He didn't mean to be naughty. He was just the most playful puppy Mandy had ever met.

The door opened, and Peter and his mum came in. Peter was holding Timmy in his arms. When the puppy saw Mandy, he began to wriggle about, barking excitedly.

"Hello, Peter, hello, Timmy," Mandy said, patting the shaggy little dog on his head. Timmy licked her fingers.

Suddenly Mandy jumped as the door burst open. A young man hurried in, carrying a bundle wrapped in a tartan blanket. He looked pale and very worried.

"I have to see the vet," he gasped. "It's very urgent."

"Of course," Jean said quickly. "What's the problem?"

"I was out in my car when I saw this poor little thing lying at the side of the road," the man explained. He gently unwrapped the blanket. "I think it must have been hit by a car."

Mrs Foster took Timmy from Peter, and he and Mandy went

over to look. *Was it a cat, or a dog?*
Mandy wondered, feeling very
worried.

No, it was a *fox*! The cub was
lying very still inside the woolly
blanket, its eyes wide open and
scared.

"Oh!" Mandy breathed.

Jean went
to get Mrs Hope.
Mandy's mum
was in the
treatment room
working at her
computer. She
hurried out and
took the injured
fox cub from the man.

"I hope he's going to be all right," the man said anxiously. "My name's Mr Graham, by the way."

"I'll take a look right away," said Mandy's mum. "You don't mind waiting, do you, Mrs Foster?"

Peter's mum shook her head. "Of course not," she replied.

"Mum, can Peter and I come in and watch?" Mandy asked.

Mrs Hope was carrying the fox cub into the treatment room. "Yes, but you must be very quiet," she told them. "It's in shock, that's why it's lying so still. And we don't want to frighten it any more."

16

Mandy, Peter and Mr Graham followed Mrs Hope into the room. Mandy watched as her mum laid the fox on the table and unwrapped the blanket.

"Oh!" Mandy gasped as Mrs Hope lifted the last fold of the blanket. "Look, Mum. Its tail's got a white tip, just like that fox cub we saw yesterday! Do you think it could be the same one?"

Chapter Three

Peter turned to Mandy, his eyes very wide. "Did you see a fox cub yesterday?" he asked. "Where?"

"We were coming back from Walton," Mandy explained. "The fox ran out into the road. The car in front of us had to stop, and so did we."

"Were you driving along Meadows Lane?" asked Mr Graham.

Mrs Hope nodded.

"Well, that's where I found him," said Mr Graham.

Mandy looked at her mum.

Mrs Hope was giving the fox an injection in his leg. "This is just to make him a bit drowsy,"

she said. "So that I can check him over without getting bitten." She gave Mr Graham some thick leather gloves. "Could you hold the fox's head to keep him very still? I must check him over to see if he's broken any bones."

"Of course," Mr Graham agreed.

Mandy and Peter watched as Mrs Hope slipped on some rubber gloves. Then she gently ran her hands over the fox's fur while Mr Graham held the fox still.

"Mum, do you think it *could* be the same one?" Mandy asked.

"I think it's quite likely," replied Mrs Hope. "Foxes like to stick to the same area. And his white-tipped tail is quite unusual."

Mandy reached out and touched the end of the cub's tail with one finger. It was the softest thing Mandy had ever felt. The fox stared back up at her with wide dark eyes.

"Will he be OK, Mum?" Mandy whispered.

"I think so," said Mrs Hope, smiling. "I can't find any broken bones, but he has some cuts and bruises. I think we'd better keep him here for a while."

"Oh, that's good news," said Mr Graham, looking relieved. "Thank you, Mrs Hope. I must go now, because I'm very late for my meeting." He said goodbye and left.

Mrs Hope took the leather gloves from him, and put them on herself. "We mustn't forget that a fox is a wild animal," she told Mandy and Peter. "He's got sharp teeth and claws. He might not mean to hurt us, but he's scared because he's in a strange place, and that might make him bite and scratch. We have to be careful."

"Are you going to put him in the wildlife treatment room?" Mandy said.

Mrs Hope nodded as she wrapped the fox in the blanket again.

"What's that?" Peter asked Mandy.

"It's a room at the back of the surgery," Mandy explained. "Wild animals have to be kept away from ordinary pets. That's because they might catch diseases from each other. Sometimes wild animals have germs that would be very dangerous to pets."

She and Peter followed Mrs Hope through the waiting room and into a large room lined with cages on shelves.

"Mandy, can you get me a clean blanket?" asked Mrs Hope. She carried the fox over to the biggest cage, while Mandy fetched a blanket from the store cupboard. She opened the door of the cage and put the blanket inside, making a cosy bed.

Then her mum gently lifted the fox on to the blanket.

"Can I stroke him?" Mandy asked.

Mrs Hope shook her head. "No, love," she replied. "We must try not to get him too used to us. Otherwise he won't be able to live in the wild when he's better."

Mandy felt a bit disappointed. But she knew that her mum was right.

"He'll be fine in a little while," said Mrs Hope. She pulled off the gloves.

"I must wash my hands. Peter, will you go and tell your mum that I'll see Timmy now?"

Peter nodded. "I hope you feel better soon!" he said to the

sleepy fox cub. "I'll see you at school tomorrow, Mandy."

Mandy smiled at him, then turned to her mother.

"Mum, can I stay with the fox for a while? He might be feeling lonely."

"All right," Mrs Hope agreed. "Just for a few minutes."

Mandy was left alone with the fox cub. She stood quietly by the cage and watched his eyes close as he fell asleep. Mandy felt very sorry for him. He was so far away from home.

"You ought to have a name," she said. "I know. I'll call you Hector."

A little tuft of Hector's fur was poking through the wire mesh of the cage. Mandy reached out and stroked it gently. "I really, really hope you feel OK tomorrow," she whispered.

Chapter Four

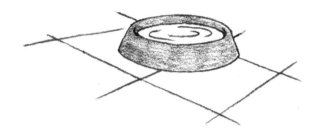

"Mum!" Mandy called. She ran across the school playground with Peter close behind her. "How's Hector?"

"He's doing very well," replied Mrs Hope.

It was the following day and school had just finished. Mandy couldn't wait to go home and see Hector again. Mrs Hope had said that Peter could come too, and stay for tea.

Mandy wriggled in her seat as her mum drove through the village. As soon as the Land-rover stopped outside Animal Ark, she and Peter jumped out.

"We can go in through the back door," said Mrs Hope as she locked the Land-rover.

"It's such a hot day that I left the door open to give Hector some air."

They walked round the side of the cottage and into the wildlife treatment room. Mandy was a bit worried that Hector might be frightened by so many people coming in all at once. But then she stopped and stared!

Hector wasn't lying down any more. He was on his feet, nosing curiously round his cage. His tail waved from side to side as he sniffed at his water bowl. Then he pawed at his blanket, grabbing it in his mouth and shaking it.

"Hector!" Mandy gasped.

The fox swung his head round at the sound of Mandy's voice. His bright dark eyes met hers.

"He's so cute," Mandy laughed. "I thought he'd be scared of us."

"No, he's quite a fearless fox!" said Mrs Hope.

"He does look a bit cheeky, doesn't he?" agreed Peter.

Hector was standing at the front of his cage. He pushed his little nose through the wire mesh, sniffing at them.

"Mum, Hector's water bowl is empty," Mandy pointed out. "Can we fill it up?"

"Yes, that's a good idea," said Mrs Hope. She pulled on her thick gloves and carefully unlatched the cage door.

Hector bounded forward to sniff at her hands as Mrs Hope took out the water bowl. She gave it to Peter,

who carried it over to the sink
and filled it with water from
the tap.

"Hector will be able to go
back to the woods in a day or
two," Mrs Hope told them,
putting the full water bowl
back into the cage. "Now, let's go
through to the kitchen and have
a snack."

"Bye, Hector," said Mandy,
waving at the fox. She couldn't
help feeling a bit sad about
Hector going away. But he was a
wild animal, not a pet, and he
belonged out in the countryside.

Mandy, Peter and Mrs Hope
went out through the waiting

room. Several people had brought their pets to see Mandy's dad, who was taking afternoon surgery. Mandy stopped to say hello to a very fluffy kitten, who purred loudly when Mandy stroked her head.

"Would you like some orange juice, Peter?" asked Mrs Hope,

leading the way into the kitchen.

"Yes, please," replied Peter. He and Mandy sat down at the table, and Mrs Hope handed them glasses of juice and bags of crisps. After a while Mr Hope came in. He was frowning.

"Did you visit Hector just now?" he asked.

"Yes," said Mandy. "What's the matter?"

"He's gone!" Mr Hope announced. "I just popped in to check on him, and his cage was empty. I don't think it was properly fastened."

Mandy jumped up. "Oh, no!" she gasped. "Quick, Peter, we must go and look for him."

Mrs Hope looked worried. "The back door of the treatment room was open," she reminded Mandy. "He might have gone out into the garden."

Mandy and Peter ran outside. Shading their eyes against the sun, they looked all round the lawn and under the bushes. But Hector was nowhere to be seen. Mandy felt tears well up in her eyes. Hector wouldn't know where he was!

"Try not to worry, love," said Mrs Hope. "Hector will be fine, even if he has gone home a day or two early."

"But won't he get lost?" Mandy asked in a wobbly voice.

Mrs Hope shook her head. "Foxes have got a great sense of smell," she explained. "Just like dogs. Hector will easily find his way home."

They went into the cottage,

and Mr Hope went back to the surgery. Mandy still felt a bit sad. She didn't feel like eating the rest of her crisps.

"Cheer up, Mandy," said Peter. "At least Hector's feeling better now."

"I know," Mandy sighed. "But I didn't even say goodbye."

BANG!

Mandy jumped. "What was that?" she said.

"It sounded like it came from the bathroom," said Mrs Hope, looking up at the ceiling.

Mandy and Peter dashed upstairs. The bathroom door was open. Mandy peeped round it. "Mum, it's Hector!" she shouted.

The little fox was having a great time exploring the Hopes' bathroom! He had already knocked over the bin. Now he was pulling the toilet roll to bits with his teeth, snarling like a puppy. There were sheets of paper all over the floor. Some of it was wrapped round Hector's tummy.

Mandy and Peter burst out laughing. Hector looked so funny.

"He's even messier than Timmy!" Peter said with a grin.

"Quick, Mandy," said Mrs Hope, hurrying upstairs and shutting the bathroom door. "Go and fetch your dad."

Mandy dashed downstairs and into the surgery. All the patients had gone, and her dad was in the waiting room with Jean. When Mr Hope heard what had happened, he grabbed the leather gloves and a travelling cage. Then they hurried back to the bathroom. Mandy, Peter and Mrs Hope watched as Mr Hope opened the door very slowly.

"Stand in the doorway so that Hector can't escape," he told Mandy and Peter.

They blocked the gap by standing close together with their hands stretched out. Inside the bathroom, Mr Hope crouched down and opened the cage. Hector began to back into the corner by the bath, his eyes bright with mischief.

"He doesn't want to go into the cage," whispered Peter.

"He's having too much fun!" Mandy said.

Wearing the thick gloves, Mr Hope reached out, picked up the fox and put him into the cage. Then he closed the door and locked it firmly. The bathroom was a mess! It looked as if a hundred Timmies had been playing in there.

"Hector, you bad boy!" Mandy laughed. She reached out and tickled the tip of the fox's tail, which was sticking through the wire.

Hector stared boldly back at

her, his eyes twinkling. He looked

as if he'd really enjoyed his little adventure!

"Well, I think it's time Hector went back to the woods," said Mr Hope with a smile. "Do you two want to come with me tomorrow when I take him home?"

"Yes, please!" said Mandy happily.

Chapter Five

"This is where Mum and I first saw Hector," Mandy explained. It was the following afternoon and they were driving down Meadows Lane. Mandy and Peter had finished school early because it was the last day of term.

"And this was where Mr Graham found him," added Peter.

"We'll drive into the woods as far as we can," Mr Hope decided.

"And then we'll let Hector go."

Mandy turned round to look at Hector. He was standing up in the travelling cage, sniffing the air and looking round.

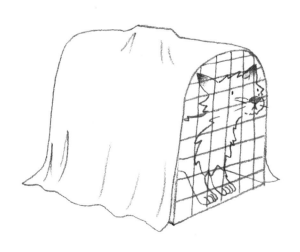

"I think Hector knows he's going home," said Peter, who was sitting beside Mandy. "He looks excited, doesn't he?"

"Yes," said Mandy. "Perhaps he can smell the woods already."

Mandy's dad turned down a bumpy track that led to a clearing in the middle of the woods. It was cool and quiet among the trees.

They all climbed out of the Land-rover and Mr Hope lifted out Hector's cage. The fox's tail brushed against the wire mesh.

Mandy reached out and touched the soft white tip for the last time.

"Stand very still," Mr Hope warned as he undid the cage.

Holding her breath, Mandy watched as Hector lifted his head. He sniffed the air, then bounded out of the cage. He ran straight towards the trees, his tail waving happily.

Suddenly he stopped. He looked over his shoulder and his dark eyes met Mandy's for a second. Then he was gone, disappearing into the ferns.

"He stopped to say thank you!" Mandy gasped, her eyes shining. "Didn't he, Dad?"

"I think he did," Mr Hope agreed with a broad smile.

"I bet Hector's really happy to be home," said Peter, as Mandy's dad picked up the cage.

"I just hope he's learned how to cross the road properly now," Mandy said. She couldn't help feeling a bit worried. Hector was so brave, he wasn't scared of *anything*, not even the busy road. She really hoped he wouldn't get into any more accidents …

Chapter Six

"I wonder where Hector is,"
Mandy said.

It was the next day, the first
day of the summer holidays.
Mandy had gone with her dad
to visit a sick sheep on a farm
near Welford. Now they were
driving home again along
Meadows Lane.

"I'm sure he's fine, wherever
he is," replied Mr Hope.

Mandy stared out of the car window. They were going through the woods where Hector lived.

Suddenly she spotted a small, reddish-brown face peeping out of

a clump of ferns at the side of the road. Next moment, a little fox

wriggled out of the leaves and on to the verge.

Mandy saw that he had a white tip at the end of his tail. "Dad, look!" she cried. "It's Hector!"

"So it is," her dad agreed. "Let's stop and watch him."

And he stopped the Land-rover at
the side of the road.

Hector stood on the grass,
staring boldly around. It looked
as if he was about to cross to the
other side.

Mandy's heart sank. A car
was coming along the road!
"Be careful, Hector!" she
whispered.

The fox pricked up his little ears as the car got closer, and turned his head to look. Mandy held her breath. Would Hector have learned his lesson after his accident?

Hector stood quietly, his tail swishing to and fro. The car slowed down when the driver spotted the fox. But still Hector did not move. He waited until the car had gone safely past. Then he ran lightly across the road and into the woods. The last Mandy saw of him was the white tip of his tail vanishing under the dark trees.

Mandy heaved a big sigh of relief. "Look, Dad!" she exclaimed.

"Hector's not just brave, he's clever, too. He's learned how to cross the road at last!"

Chapter One

"Mum! Look! There's Helen!" said Mandy Hope, pointing out of the Land-rover window.

Helen Cook, one of Mandy's friends from school, was jumping up and down outside the old stone farmhouse where she lived. She had a *huge* smile on her face.

"She looks even more excited than you," laughed Mrs Hope, as she parked the Land-rover.

Helen's pony, Bluebell, had given birth to a foal just three days ago. Mrs Hope had come to check mother and baby over. Both Mandy's parents were vets, which was great for Mandy because she was mad about animals! Sometimes she got to go on her mum's visits, especially in the summer holidays. Today, Helen had invited Mandy to stay at Willow Farm all day.

Mandy undid her seat belt and clambered out of the car as fast as she could.

"Mandy!" Helen burst out, running up to her. "You are going to *love* Fern. She is the sweetest foal in the whole world!"

Mandy and Helen ran inside to say hello to Mrs Cook, while Mandy's mum got her vet's bag out of the car.

"Lemon squash, Mandy?" smiled Mrs Cook.

"Oh yes, please," said Mandy. "Where's Fern?"

"She's in a pen with Bluebell," said Helen, as Mrs Hope came in with her bag. "Dad made it specially. Bluebell's stable isn't really big enough for the two of them. Fern likes to run around already!"

"But she's only three days old!" Mandy gasped.

"In the wild, foals need to run when they're a few *hours* old," said Mrs Hope. "If they couldn't, other animals like wolves would gobble them up!"

"Well, Fern would *definitely* be able to run away," said Helen proudly. "By the time we move to Dorset, she'll be able to run faster than me!"

"I expect she can already," Mrs Hope said with a smile.

The Cooks were moving to Dorset soon. Mandy was sad that they were going, but there was still time for her to get to know Fern before they went. She couldn't wait to see her! She drank her squash in one big gulp. Then she and her mum followed Helen and Mrs Cook out to the barn.

As Mrs Cook opened the barn

door, Mandy peered inside. Bluebell stood knee-deep in straw, munching a mouthful of hay. And there beside her was Fern.

"Oh!" said Mandy in surprise. "She's black and white!"

"Yes," said Helen. "She looks like her dad. Isn't she *lovely*?"

Mandy had expected the foal to look like Bluebell. Helen's pony was a pretty grey colour, which Helen said was called blue roan. But Fern was white with big black patches. Her mane and tail were black and fluffy.